To Michael and Scott, still my bunnies
—C. F.

𝒜
atheneum

ATHENEUM BOOKS FOR YOUNG READERS
An imprint of Simon & Schuster Children's Publishing Division
1230 Avenue of the Americas, New York, New York 10020
Text copyright © 2014 by Candace Fleming
Illustrations copyright © 2014 by G. Brian Karas
ATHENEUM BOOKS FOR YOUNG READERS is a registered trademark of Simon & Schuster, Inc.
Atheneum logo is a trademark of Simon & Schuster, Inc.
For information about special discounts for bulk purchases, please contact Simon & Schuster
Special Sales at 1-866-506-1949 or business@simonandschuster.com.
The Simon & Schuster Speakers Bureau can bring authors to your live event. For more
information or to book an event, contact the Simon & Schuster Speakers Bureau at
1-866-248-3049 or visit our website at www.simonspeakers.com.
Book design by Ann Bobco
The text for this book is set in KosmikOT.
The illustrations for this book are rendered in gouache and acrylic with pencil.
Manufactured in China
0114 SCP
First Edition
2 4 6 8 10 9 7 5 3 1
Library of Congress Cataloging-in-Publication Data
Fleming, Candace.
Tippy-tippy-tippy, splash! / Candace Fleming ; illustrated by G. Brian Karas. — 1st ed.
p. cm
Summary: Fed up with the constant presence of rabbits in his house and yard, Mr. McGreely
goes to the beach for some fun but the pesky pufftails will not give him a break.
ISBN 978-1-4169-5403-3 (hardcover)
ISBN 978-1-4814-0028-2 (eBook)
[1. Rabbits—Fiction. 2. Beaches—Fiction.] I. Karas, G. Brian, illustrator. II. Title.
PZ7.F59936Tiv 2014
[E]—dc23
2012051496

Candace Fleming

Tippy-Tippy-Tippy, Splash!

illustrated by G. Brian Karas

atheneum

Atheneum Books for Young Readers

New York London Toronto Sydney New Delhi

Mr. McGreely had bunny problems.

He had bunnies in his garden.

Bunnies in his shed.

Bunnies in his cupboard.

Bunnies in his . . . BED!

"I can't take it anymore!" bellowed Mr. McGreely.
"I need a break. I need to escape.
I need a day at—

THE BEACH!"

Mr. McGreely grinned as his idea grew.

"What fun!" he exclaimed. "I will search for shells,
fly a kite in the sky, surf on the waves,
and build a big, tall sand castle.
Best of all, there won't be a pesky pufftail in sight."

So, bright and early the next morning, Mr. McGreely
packed his surfboard and snorkel, his sand pail and shovel.
Then he bustled off to put on his bathing suit.
And . . .

tippy-tippy-tippy, pat!
Click-clack-snap!

Minutes later, Mr. McGreely slid into the driver's seat.
"Good-bye, bunnies!" he called out. "Hello, fun!"
He hummed a snappy, happy tune all the way to the beach.

Once there, he spread out his blanket
and flopped onto his belly.
"Ah," he sighed. "Let the fun begin."
But . . .

Tippy-tippy-tippy, pat!

Flip-plop-flop!

When Mr. McGreely saw the three little bunnies
sunbathing on his blanket, he was angry.

"Oh no!" he exclaimed. "No bunny—nohow, noway—
is sharing my fun day."
He stomped away in search of shells.

SIFT

SIFT

POKE

LOOK

LIFT!

He uncovered half a sand dollar and two cracked clamshells.
"By golly, that was fun!" exclaimed Mr. McGreely.
"And just look what I found!"

He skipped back to his blanket.

Meanwhile . . .

Tippy-tippy-tippy, grab!
Plucked from the sand.
Tippy-nab.

Three little bunnies combing for shells,
dragging a sack as big as themselves.

Ooomph!

When Mr. McGreely saw the three little bunnies' big heap
of sea treasures, he was REALLY angry.
"Trying to show me up, eh?" he sputtered.

"Well, let's see you wily twitchwhiskers do THIS."
Grabbing a kite, he ran up and down, up and down the beach.

HUFF HUFF GASP PANT

PUFF!

The kite bounced along behind.

"By golly, that was really fun," Mr. McGreely wheezed happily.
"And my kite even lifted off for a second." He headed back to his blanket.

Meanwhile . . .

Tippy-tippy-tippy, dash!

Down the shoreline. **Tippy-flash.**

Three little bunnies flying a kite, clutching the string with all of their might. **Wheeeee!**

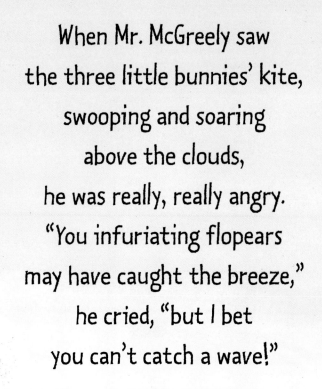

When Mr. McGreely saw
the three little bunnies' kite,
swooping and soaring
above the clouds,
he was really, really angry.
"You infuriating flopears
may have caught the breeze,"
he cried, "but I bet
you can't catch a wave!"

And tucking a surfboard
under his arm,
he sprinted across the sand,
dove into the surf,
and . . .

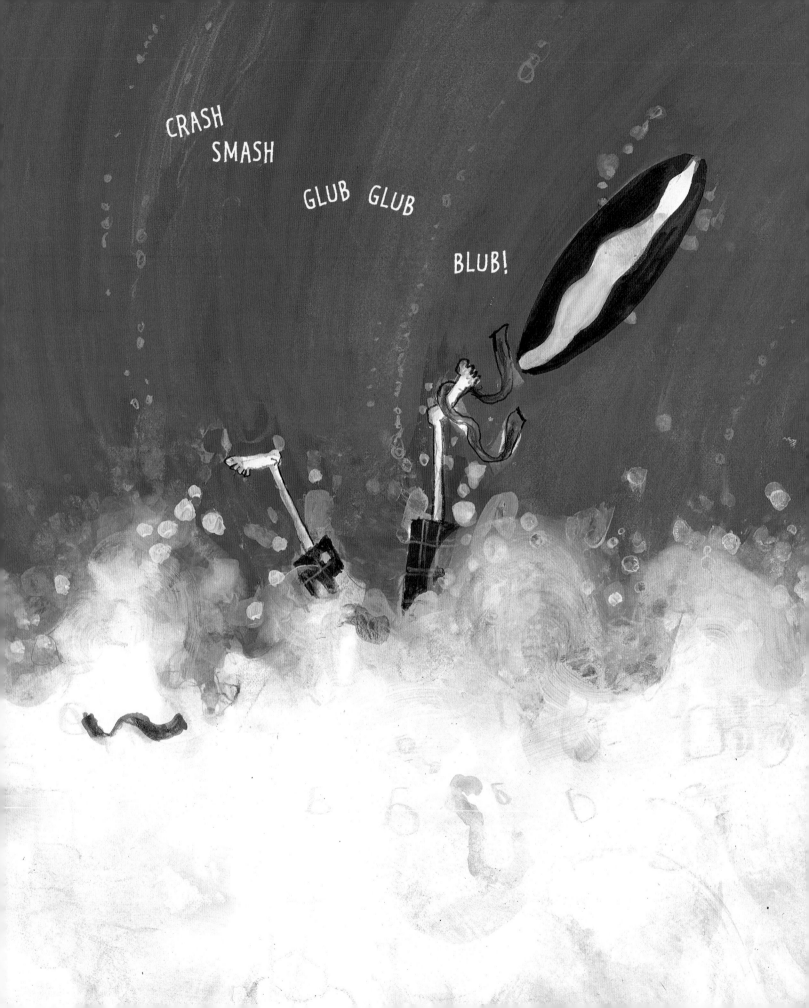

He washed ashore, spitting and sputtering.
"Fun," Mr. McGreely coughed.

He dripped back to his blanket.

Meanwhile . . .

Tippy-tippy-tippy, dash!
Riding the waves.
Tippy-splash.

Three little bunnies glide onshore, then giggle and wiggle

and splash back for more.

Cowa-bunnies!

When Mr. McGreely saw
the three little bunnies shooting the curls
and riding the waves, he was—

FURIOUS!

"Blast you wily twitchwhiskers!" he shouted.
"You want to see fun? I'll show you fun!"

Snatching up a pail and shovel,
he stormed down the beach to
the sand castle contest.

"First prize wins lunch at the
Veggie Hut," said the judge.

Sand Castle Contest

Mr. McGreely dropped to his knees in the sand.
"By golly," he fumed. "Let's see those four-pawed show-offs do THIS."
And he started building, but . . .

CRUMBLE

TUMBLE

PLOP

PLOP

SLOP!

All he could make was a mound of wet sand.
"So much for my fun day," sniffled Mr. McGreely. He wiped a tear away.

But then . . . tippy-tippy-tippy—

TA-DA!

Mr. McGreely looked from the bunnies
to the other castles
then back to the bunnies.
"Well, maybe," he finally said,
"just this once."

So together they shoveled and shaped, scooped and caked, molded and piled
and patted and raked. And they built a big, tall sand castle.
It was decorated with seashells. A bright kite fluttered
from one of its towers. And a surfboard served as a drawbridge.

"The winner!" declared the judge.
He slapped a blue ribbon onto the castle
and a gift certificate into Mr. McGreely's hand.

Mr. McGreely grinned.
"Now THAT," he exclaimed, "was fun!"

Muncha, muncha, muncha!